Sir Winston Walrus

and

THE GREAT RESCUE

A Sea World Book ™

© 1994 Sea World, Inc. All Rights Reserved

Sea World, the Whale Logo, and the Sea World Characters are trademarks of Sea World, Inc.
No part of this book may be reproduced or copied in any form or by any means —
graphics, electronic, or mechanical, including photo copying, taping, or information storage and
retrieval systems — without written permission of the publisher.

Published by

THIRD STORY BOOKS™

955 Connecticut Avenue, Suite 1302

Bridgeport, Connecticut 06607

ISBN 1-884506-06-2

Distributed to the trade by

Andrews & McMeel

4900 Main Street

Kansas City, Missouri 64112

Library of Congress Catalog Card Number: 93-61825

Printed in Singapore

Sir Winston Walrus

and THE GREAT RESCUE

A book about discovery (geography) by ELAINE LONERGAN

Illustrated by WILLIAM LANGLEY STUDIOS

THIRD™ STORY BOOKS

Dear Grown-up:

When SEA WORLD opened its doors in 1964, it had a mission. That mission was to give adults and children a chance to see and learn about all the creatures of the sea . . . and to help preserve these creatures for future generations.

SEA WORLD books have a similar mission. They were created to entertain, and to help teach children something about the wonderful creatures that call the oceans home. And all books in this series are approved by the Education Department at SEA WORLD.

But SEA WORLD books teach kids other things, too—such as the importance of friendship, of self-esteem, of caring for our planet and for one another. Most importantly, SEA WORLD books accomplish their "missions" by telling stories about the wonderful creatures of the sea— stories your children will love to experience again and again.

By the way, when you've finished reading the story in this SEA WORLD book, don't forget to take a look at the two pages that follow the story. On them are some seaworthy facts about things in the story that you and your children might find interesting.

Welcome to SEA WORLD books. We hope your whole family enjoys them . . . and learns a little something from them, too!

Sincerely,
The Publishers

It was a beautiful and sunny day. Once again, Sir Winston Walrus had Virgil Pelican hard at work. "Come on, there. Heave ho. Get a move on," Sir Winston barked at Virgil, who was carrying a load of thatch in his bill.

"Good job, mate," Sir Winston said to Virgil who had safely landed. "That ought to be enough to repair the hole in my roof. We'll be shipshape by tonight."

"Now can you finish your story about your trip to the South Seas?" asked Virgil. You see, whenever Virgil worked for Sir Winston, he was rewarded with a story about one of the sea captain's many adventures.

"Ahhh. . .what a life I've had," Sir Winston sighed. "But you know, Virgil, you've yet to tell me a story about any of *your* travels."

"That's because I've never had a *real* adventure, not like yours. I'm a pelican without a story to tell," Virgil said sadly.

Meanwhile, down the beach, Seamore and Clyde Sea Lion were taking turns diving into the water.

"One, two, three, I'm splashing in the sea," Seamore sang happily as he dove.

"Four, five, six, I'm swimming just for kicks," Clyde called as he jumped in to join Seamore.

While they were sliding, spinning, and twirling through the water, the two sea lions noticed Clancy Clam clapping his shell open and shut. Clyde and Seamore quickly swam to Clancy's side.

"What's the word?" Clyde asked.

"I've heard through a line of clams that there's a baby seal who's hurt in a far-away ocean," Clancy told them. "But I don't know what ocean he's in."

"I'll tell Shamu," Seamore said quickly. "Clyde, you go tell Sir Winston. They'll know what to do."

Seamore found Shamu, Baby Shamu, and Sydney the Shark visiting Dolly Dolphin.

"That's awful!" cried Baby Shamu when Seamore told them about the seal.

"Don't worry," Shamu told Seamore. "We'll sail to the rescue with Sir Winston at the helm of the FunShip."

"We must set sail immediately," Sir Winston said when he heard Clancy's news. "We'll head to the Pacific Ocean first. Now, let's hurry!"

At that very moment, Shamu rose to the surface, his spout spraying a stream of mist. "Baby Shamu, Sydney, Dolly and I will follow once you set sail," he told Sir Winston.

The FunShip sailed for many a day. At last, the Crew spotted the warm blue waters of the Pacific.

"We must find out if our baby seal is here," said Dolly. "Virgil, could you look around?"

Virgil took off from the mast and soared over the ocean.

Virgil flew far and wide, but he found no sign of the baby seal. Finally, he perched on a rock and addressed a school of albacore.

"There's a baby seal stranded somewhere," he told them. "He's hurt and alone. Have you seen him?"

"We've just traveled far and wide, but we saw no sign of a hurt baby seal," replied the school in albacore harmony.

After Virgil flew back to the ship, Sir Winston took out his charts.
"We're heading for the Southern Ocean, mateys. All hands on deck!"
And so the FunShip set sail once again.

After many days and nights, the FunShip reached the cold waters where the Atlantic, Pacific, and Indian Oceans meet.

"Virgil," instructed Sir Winston. "could you find our old friends, Pete and Penny Penguin? Perhaps they've seen the baby seal."

Virgil took off once again. He shivered with the cold, and tiny icicles formed on his wings. But finally, he found Pete and Penny, lounging on an iceberg.

"Virgil!" cried Pete. "Nice to see you. What are you doing down here?"
"I'm looking for a hurt baby seal," chattered Virgil. "Have you seen him?"
"How terrible!" said Penny. "Poor thing. But he isn't anywhere near here.
You'd better head north."

"Where are we off to now?" Virgil asked when he returned to the FunShip.

"We're charting a course to the Indian Ocean, where coral reefs dot the sea and sunken ships clutter the deep," Sir Winston said, with a glimmer of days past in his eyes.

Virgil sighed. *If only I had adventures like Sir Winston*, he thought sadly.

Days passed. Nights passed. And then, the FunShip and its hardy crew sailed into the waters of the warm Indian Ocean.

"Look!" called Virgil, who was flying overhead to scout out the terrain. "The water is so clear that I can see a sunken ship! It looks very old!"

"See if you can spot our baby seal," Shamu suggested.

On a far-off beach, Virgil met a wise old lobster.
"Have you seen a hurt baby seal?" Virgil asked him.
"Not around here," the lobster said, clicking its claws.

When Virgil returned and told the crew what had happened, a big tear fell down Baby Shamu's cheek.

"Will we ever find that poor baby seal?" he whispered.

"Of course we will," said Shamu. "Virgil is doing a great job. Where are we headed next, Sir Winston?"

"To the Atlantic! Sir Winston ordered. "Man your stations. It's full speed ahead!"

Around the coast of Africa and up the southern Atlantic sailed the FunShip and its troubled crew.

There was a storm brewing in the Atlantic. Waves crashed. Soon the rain began to fall.

"See what you can spy!" said Sir Winston to Virgil. And the brave pelican took off once again.

This time, luck was with him. Down below, on a tiny rock in the middle of the giant storm, was a tiny baby seal.

Virgil flew back to the ship and told the crew what he had seen.

"What can we do?" asked Baby Shamu.

"I don't know," Shamu admitted. "The storm is getting stronger. None of us can swim to the rock, and we can't let the FunShip get near it or she might be dashed to pieces."

The crew thought and thought. But it was Virgil who finally came up with a plan.

"I can try to fly the seal to safety," he said.

For the last time, Virgil took off from the FunShip. He flew to the baby seal's side. Then he carefully picked up the seal in his bill and carried him to a rocky shore where a family of seals lived. The FunShip followed behind.

"You did it!" cheered Baby Shamu. "Virgil rescued the baby seal!"
"Thank you," whispered the baby seal. "You're my hero."
Virgil just blushed. He had never felt so good in all his life.

"More thatch!" Sir Winston bellowed. "Virgil, we need more thatch. There's another hole in the roof!"

Virgil dropped a giant load of thatch on Sir Winston's roof.

"Have I ever told you the story of the time I rescued a hurt baby seal from the middle of the Atlantic Ocean?" he asked Sir Winston.

Sir Winston smiled. "I don't think so," he said.

And so Virgil began his tale. And he's been telling it ever since.

Ahoy, There!

This is Shamu...and here
are some seaworthy facts for you!

Sailing the Seven Seas

Many years ago, when sailors talked about sailing the seven seas, they meant sailing all of the oceans around the world. These days, we know that there are many more seas than seven. But there are only five actual oceans on the globe. In this story, the FunShip sailed through the Pacific Ocean, the Atlantic Ocean, the Indian Ocean, and the Southern Ocean (also known as the Antarctic Ocean). There was just one ocean that the FunShip didn't get to. Do you know which it was? *The Arctic Ocean.*

Seal of Approval

The FunShip was trying to rescue a baby seal in this story. But Shamu and his Crew aren't the only ones trying to rescue baby seals.

In 1972, the U.S. Marine Mammal Protection Act made it illegal to hunt or harass any marine mammal in U.S. waters. This included seals and walruses. One of the major exceptions to this rule is that scientists and oceanaria like SEA WORLD can display marine mammals for research, for humane purposes, and for education. This allows people to learn about these animals and about how we can help them survive.

FISH STORY

In their search for the injured seal, the FunShip crew saw many different sea creatures that they had never seen before. Here are some that live in the oceans they visited.

Pacific Ocean

SALMON: an oceanic fish that moves to streams to breed.

TUNA: a fast-swimming ocean fish that lives in large schools.

BILLFISH: a fish that has a long, slender jaw like a bird's beak.

ALBACORE: a kind of tuna with long pectoral fins.

Southern (Antarctic) Ocean

PETREL: a small-to-medium-sized bird that lives near the water and feeds on small fish.

ALBATROSS: another bird that lives near the water, the albatross is related to the petrel but is much larger.

Indian Ocean

TURTLE: a reptile that has a hard shell on its back.

PARROT FISH: a fish with teeth that are connected to its parrot-like bill.

BARRACUDA: known for their giant appetites, barracudas live in warm waters. Some barracudas are poisonous.

Sea World®

"For in the end we will conserve only what we love.
We will love only what we understand.
And we will understand only what we are taught."

Baba Dioum — noted Central African Naturalist

Since the first Sea World opened in 1964, more than 160 million people have experienced first-hand the majesty and mystery of marine life. Sea World parks have been leaders in building public understanding and appreciation for killer whales, dolphins, and a vast variety of other sea creatures.

Through its work in animal rescue and rehabilitation, breeding, animal care, research and education, Sea World demonstrates a strong commitment to the preservation of marine life and the environment.

Sea World provides all its animals with the highest-quality care including state-of-the-art facilities and stimulating positive reinforcement training programs. Each park employs full-time veterinarians, trainers, biologists and other animal care experts to provide 24-hour care. Through close relationships with these animals — relationships that are built on trust — Sea World's animal care experts are able to monitor their health every day to ensure their well-being. In short, all animals residing at Sea World are treated with respect, love and care.

If you would like more information about Sea World books, please write to us. We'd like to hear from you.

THIRD STORY BOOKS
955 Connecticut Avenue, Suite 1302
Bridgeport, CT 06607